SURVIVAL
Avalanche!

Frieda Wishinsky

Illustrated by
Norman Lanting

Scholastic Canada Ltd.

Toronto New York London Auckland Sydney
Mexico City New Delhi Hong Kong Buenos Aires

Scholastic Canada Ltd.
604 King Street West, Toronto, Ontario M5V 1E1, Canada

Scholastic Inc.
557 Broadway, New York, NY 10012, USA

Scholastic Australia Pty Limited
PO Box 579, Gosford, NSW 2250, Australia

Scholastic New Zealand Limited
Private Bag 94407, Botany, Manukau 2163, New Zealand

Scholastic Children's Books
Euston House, 24 Eversholt Street, London NW1 1DB, UK

www.scholastic.ca

Library and Archives Canada Cataloguing in Publication
Wishinsky, Frieda, author
    Avalanche! / Frieda Wishinsky.
(Survival)
Issued in print and electronic formats.
ISBN 978-1-4431-4638-8 (pbk.).--ISBN 978-1-4431-4639-5 (ebook).--
ISBN 978-1-4431-4640-1 (Apple edition)
    I. Title. II. Series: Wishinsky, Frieda Survival.
PS8595.I834A9 2015   jC813'.54   C2015-901887-0
                                          C2015-901888-9

Many thanks to Judy and Cory Green and Tamara Sztainbok.

6 5 4 3 2 1   Printed in Canada 121   15 16 17 18 19

MIX
Paper from
responsible sources
FSC FSC® C004071
www.fsc.org

For Diane Kerner, with thanks

CHAPTER ONE

February 15

Finally, thought Alex. *A perfect day for a snow fort.* Snow covered everything. It blanketed the roof of the old three-storey house. It whitened the tops of the rickety wooden shed and the black garbage cans at the side of the yard. It coated the branches of the skinny pine trees in the back and the towering maple at the front. Most striking of all, it enveloped Mount Ava, the tall, jagged mountain right behind Alex's house. The mountain looked like a giant wrapped in a white fur coat.

It had snowed for three days straight but now the sun sparkled. The air was crisp and cold but there was no wind. The firm, slightly wet snow was just right for building a fort. And now that Owen had joined them, they might finish the fort before dark.

They were working so hard on the last wall of the fort that at first only Alex heard the rumble. He looked up as the noise grew louder. Closer. It sounded like a speeding train but there were no trains in Glory.

"Did you hear that?" he asked.

"Yeah. I heard something," said Owen. "They're probably dynamiting on the road. They do that to stop avalanches from crashing down near the highway."

"That boom isn't down the road. It's close. Really close. It's like thunder. It's like . . . Owen! Ben! Look!"

Alex pointed up to Mount Ava.

Waves of snow barrelled down the mountain, breaking branches, crushing trees, pumping out blinding clouds of snow — heading right for them.

"Avalanche!" shouted Alex. "Run!"

But they couldn't run.

The force of the fast-moving snow knocked them off their feet.

2

CHAPTER TWO

One month earlier

Alex gripped the hard grey arm of the sofa. He stared at the images on the TV screen as the documentary narrator's voice filled their darkened living room.

"Snow roared down the mountain engulfing everything in its path. People screamed and ran — desperate for safety and cover. But the avalanche was too powerful. Too fast. It buried them under mounds of heavy snow. Some even died while asleep in their tents. And then the snow stopped. There was a ghostly silence. It was over."

Alex took a long, deep breath. He brushed his

straight-as-a-ruler brown hair out of his eyes and pushed his black glasses up his nose.

It's not real. It all happened long ago, he told himself. *It's just a reenactment of something that happened over a hundred years ago.*

So why did it feel so real? Maybe because they were now living close to steep mountains in Glory, British Columbia. Glory was close to the Rockies and to Jasper and Glacier National Parks. There were avalanche warning signs all along the highway, but until tonight Alex hadn't worried. He liked mountains. They sparkled in the sun, peeked through thick fog and shimmered like cathedrals on clear, star-lit nights.

"Parks Canada still warns hikers to equip themselves with shovels, avalanche transceivers and probes so they can be located if caught in an avalanche." Alex shuddered at the historian's last words.

His dad flicked on the lights. "So what do you think?" he asked.

"What an amazing story, Luc. It's going to make a great book," said Alex's mom. "I can't wait to visit the Yukon this summer. It will be amazing to see where the Gold Rush actually took place."

"Is there still gold there?" asked Emma. Alex's nine-year-old sister looked up at her dad with a mischievous look in her brown eyes.

"Probably not," said his Dad. "But we can check it out."

Alex's dad was a writer. He was writing a historical novel set in the Yukon, during the Gold Rush. They were planning a family trip to the Yukon in July so his dad could get a first-hand look at the landscape he was describing.

"Could an avalanche happen here?" asked Emma. She didn't look scared, just curious. But Alex was glad she asked the question and not him.

"You've seen those snow sheds on the highway — those structures that look like small bridges built into the mountain? They help protect drivers from avalanches," said Dad. "And anyway most avalanches occur in the backcountry."

"But what about Mount Ava?" said Emma.

"There's never been an avalanche on Mount Ava. Probably because it's restricted to winter sports to protect the elk herds up there. There's little chance of an avalanche."

"Let's have hot chocolate," said his mom. "That'll warm us up after all this talk of avalanches."

While his mom and Emma headed to the kitchen, Alex peered out the big picture window in the living room. The snow had finally stopped, but more was expected to fall. Maybe there'd finally be enough snow to build a snow fort. The snow was piling up on tall, spiky Mount Ava and all over the yard. It already covered the trees, the bushes and the bird feeder.

Alex couldn't wait to build a snow fort. His dad
had promised to help him but he was busy with
his book. He'd spent the three months since they

first arrived in Glory researching online and at the small Glory library. He told Alex he'd try and help him build a fort in February, but February was two weeks away.

Emma said she'd help too, but Alex couldn't count on her. She always got bored before they were even halfway through. It was Sam he needed, Sam he counted on, but Sam was back in Halifax.

Sam and Alex were best friends and expert snow fort builders. Sam would have loved the snow in Glory. He would have also loved Alex's room in the attic with its sloping ceiling and its window facing the mountain. It wasn't a big house but it had lots of hidden nooks and deep cupboards. It also had a big wide porch in the back with four red rocking chairs.

Alex's room was more fun than his small bedroom in Halifax. The only view from his Halifax window was the neighbour's brick wall.

If only he weren't so lonely in Glory. It was hard

to make friends at school. The kids in his class weren't mean, except for Owen Slater and Owen's buddy Nate Mendes. They kept snickering and calling him "New Boy." As for the rest of the kids — they'd all known each other since kindergarten. Alex was the new kid. Worse — he was the new kid from out East.

Unlike Alex, in Glory everyone knew how to ski or snowboard. Lots of families had snowmobiles and zipped around the trails on the weekends. As for hockey — Alex had wobbly ankles, so he wasn't good at that.

But he was great at snow forts. He wanted to be an architect when he grew up, and he liked all kinds of buildings. But snow forts were his favourite. The kids back in Halifax called Alex and Sam the "Fort Kings."

Alex's mom carried out a tray of mugs filled with steaming hot chocolate. Emma passed around a plate of their mom's peanut butter chocolate chip cookies — Alex's favourite. His mom was a pastry chef and had her dream job at the Glory Mountain Resort and Spa, a sprawling, luxury resort that drew people from all over the world.

Alex bit into a cookie. His mom's cookies were as delicious as ever. If only he were sharing them with Sam. If only Sam were there. Then Glory would feel like home.

CHAPTER THREE

At ten o'clock Alex climbed into bed, pulled the soft green and white quilt up to his chest and opened his new book. It was called *My Friend The Alien* and it was about two boys, Jan and Michael, who discovered an alien in their backyard. The night before he'd laughed out loud when the boys tried to talk to the alien. But tonight, before Alex could finish a page, his mind drifted back to the documentary. *Why did we have to watch it?* Now he couldn't get avalanches out of his mind.

Stop worrying, he told himself. *There's no chance of an avalanche here.*

Alex opened his book and tried to read again. Soon he was laughing — especially when the alien spoke to Jan and Michael in rhyming English:

> I am from far away.
>
> Don't know how long I'll stay.
>
> I hope it is okay
>
> to sleep in your room today.

"Alex, lights out. School tomorrow," called his mom. "Don't make five minutes turn into ten or twenty. It's late."

They went through the five-minute routine every night. His mom knew that if he was reading a good book, it was hard for him to stop.

Fifteen minutes later his mom poked her head into his room.

"Alex . . ."

"Okay. I'm turning off my light."

Alex flipped off the old brass lamp beside his bed. Then he turned to his side, pulled the quilt over his shoulder and was soon sound asleep.

* * *

The next thing he knew he was running, tripping, falling — a mountain of snow speeding behind him.

No! I'm going to be buried alive. I have to escape. But he couldn't escape. The snow catapulted him over bumps and ridges. It tossed him into a crevasse. He was . . . *No!*

Alex opened his eyes. His heart was pounding but he wasn't buried in snow. He was in his own bed. He hadn't been caught in an avalanche.

Phew! It was only a nightmare.

Alex yanked his quilt higher. He tried to push the image of the avalanche out of his mind. He looked at the clock beside his bed. It was 6:00 a.m. He still had an hour to sleep.

He tossed from side to side but it was useless, he couldn't sleep. He sat up and turned on his light. He slipped out of bed, walked over to the computer on his desk and googled "avalanche."

The first entry was terrifying — a video of a real avalanche thundering down a mountain. The skier who filmed it had almost been buried alive. She'd been rescued, but it was a close call.

Alex scrolled down to an article about avalanches. His dad was right. Unlike the late 1800s, these days in North America avalanches almost always occurred in the backcountry. Then again, in far off countries, avalanches did hit communities. In 1962 an avalanche from Huascaran, the highest mountain in Peru, killed thousands. And then there was an avalanche that hit a village in Austria in 1999 and buried 57 people — many of them died.

Alex scrolled down farther. He read about two skiers who were caught in an avalanche in the backcountry not far from Glory a few years ago. One died. The other survived. The one who survived was lucky. She was found quickly. The article said time was critical. When someone is buried in the snow for more than ten minutes, the snow starts to weigh down like cement and makes it hard to breathe.

Alex was about to read more when he heard his mother's footsteps. "Are you up, Alex?"

"I'll be right there." He shut off his computer and straightened the quilt on his bed. He slipped on his new jeans and a blue shirt, ran a comb through his hair and headed downstairs for breakfast.

His mom was alone in the kitchen. "Good morning. Want some cereal?"

"Sure," said Alex

"We'll have to get moving," said his mom. "The school bus isn't running this morning because of the icy roads. I'll give you and Emma a lift, but it's going to be a long, slow ride."

CHAPTER FOUR

The temperature had climbed overnight and instead of snow, ice clung to everything — the streets, the trees, the electric wires, the houses and the cars. Long icicles hung from their roof like sharp knives. It took Alex, Emma and their mom ten minutes to scrape the thick ice off their car.

"We'd better go," said his mom. Alex slid into the back seat beside Emma.

His mom took a deep breath, exhaled and turned on the ignition.

Cars skidded along the roads and the highway. Alex's mom gripped the steering wheel as she drove. Emma read in the back. No one said a word even when they passed two smashed-up cars in a ditch. The twenty-minute drive felt like two hours.

Finally they reached the school. Alex's mom leaned back against the car seat. She closed her eyes, took another deep breath and exhaled. "What a drive. I hope the roads are better when I pick you up. Thank goodness I only have a few blocks to drive to work."

Emma and Alex got out of the car and walked to the front door as their mom slowly drove off. School was quieter than usual. They passed the office. The secretary and vice-principal were just taking off their coats, but the principal hadn't arrived yet. Lots of people were going to be late.

"See you later, Alex," said Emma skipping down the hall to her class.

Emma's class was beside the library on the first floor. Her teacher was there. As soon as Alex neared his classroom, he knew his teacher,

Mr. Moore, was not. Kids were screaming. Paper airplanes flew into the hall. Alex slipped off his boots outside his classroom. There was a smaller than usual lineup of boots and shoes. He walked into the class.

"Hey, you! New Boy!" Owen called. Owen and Nate were folding paper airplanes. "I thought you'd be too chicken to come to school today. I bet Halifax kids don't have to deal with ice like this."

"We've had ice storms," said Alex. "We have snow and cold weather. It's just different in Halifax because there's more traffic and no mountains."

Owen rolled his eyes. "Yeah, different's the word." He poked Nate in the arm. Alex headed to the back of the room to hang up his jacket. But before he could, Owen yanked his blue hat off and tossed it to Nate.

"Give it back," said Alex.

"Make me," said Owen.

All the kids in the room looked up.

Alex's heart raced. He took a step toward Nate and then he stopped. "You know what. Keep the hat. I have a better one at home, and my sister wore this one when she had a cold last week. It's probably full of germs."

"I don't believe you," said Owen.

"Me neither," said Nate.

"I don't care if you believe me," said Alex. He hung up his jacket and walked to his seat in the second row. He pulled out a book and began to read.

Nate sauntered over to Alex. He dropped Alex's hat on his desk. "Here. Take your germy hat."

Alex didn't take his eyes off his book. "Thanks."

Owen aimed a paper airplane at Alex, but it flew out the door and hit Mr. Moore as he was walking into class. Mr. Moore crumpled the plane and tossed it into the recycle bin. "Back to your seats. I want you to meet a new member of our class. Come in, Ben."

A boy with curly blond hair followed Mr. Moore into the class. "Ben Green and his dad just moved to Glory from Los Angeles, California. Let's welcome them warmly, especially since this weather must be a shock after sunny LA. Ben, grab a seat."

Ben hung up his jacket and sat down in the third row bechind Alex. Alex turned in his seat. "Hi," he said.

Ben grinned. "Hi."

"It looks like we'll have indoor recess later," said Mr. Moore. "Alex, could you show Ben what books we're using and fill him in on our work during recess?"

"Sure," said Alex.

❋   ❋   ❋

After social studies and journal writing, the recess bell rang. Alex pulled out his books to show Ben. "What was it like living in LA?" he asked.

"Warm and sunny most of the time. The ocean and mountains are close, but it never feels wintery. We lived in LA for four years. We're originally from upstate New York."

"There's a lot of snow in New York State, right?"

"A lot. I used to build snow forts with my dad. Then we moved to LA for his job."

"How come you moved to Glory?"

Ben cleared his throat. "Mom died last year. Dad thought we needed to get away."

"I'm sorry about your mom," said Alex.

Ben bit his lip. "Thanks. Mom was sick for most of last year. When the offer to be assistant manager at the resort here in Glory came through, Dad said yes."

"My mom works at the resort. She's the head pastry chef."

"Does she bring pastries home?" asked Ben, grinning.

"Sometimes. And sometimes she bakes at home.

You have to taste her peanut butter and chocolate chip cookies. They're amazing."

"I love peanut butter and chocolate chip cookies!"

"Maybe you could come over and try her cookies and then we could build a snow fort."

Ben grinned. "That would be great. Dad and I built a tree house last year. It's been so long since I built a snow fort."

The bell rang. Recess was over. Alex scribbled his phone number on a piece of paper and gave it to Ben. Ben wrote his number down for Alex.

Alex smiled as he tucked Ben's number into his jeans pocket. Maybe he'd finally made a friend in Glory.

CHAPTER FIVE

Alex couldn't wait for ten o'clock. Ben was coming over for the first time and they were going to build their first snow fort. They'd talked about it every day at recess. They'd each made a picture of their ideal snow fort. Alex wanted a tall one, like a teepee. Ben wanted a low, wide one, like a tunnel. They'd combined both their ideas and decided to make their fort medium height and wide, like an igloo.

They'd have at least seven hours of light to build. It had snowed all Friday night and the snow was heavy and wet, perfect for snow bricks. It was a perfect day all around. The sun was shining. The sky was clear blue. The air was crisp but not windy.

And the snow on the mountains was glistening like jewels.

At ten o'clock Ben's dad drove up to the Masons' house. Alex's mom and dad invited Ben and his dad inside for coffee, milk and buttermilk scones.

"Everyone at the resort says your pastries are delicious, Nora," said Ben's dad as he took a second bite of a scone smeared with thick English cream and raspberry jam. "But now I know they are."

"They're great, Mrs. Mason," said Ben.

"Thanks!" said Alex's mom. "But why are you boys eating so fast?"

"We want to get outside and start building," said Alex. "We have a lot to do."

"And the weather report said there's a thirty percent chance of freezing rain late in the afternoon," said Ben.

"So we want to finish in case it comes down."

"Good luck, boys," said Alex's mom.

The boys slurped down their milk and gobbled

up the rest of their scones. Then they hurried outside. Alex pulled out four plastic containers, three metal shovels and two long wooden sticks from the shed. Ben and Alex started filling the buckets and tubs with snow.

"Can I help?" asked Emma, skipping out in her furry winter boots.

"Here," said Alex, passing her a container and shovel. "Fill it to the top with snow. Pat it down and then dump the snow brick near the side of the house. We're drawing the shape of the fort."

"Okay," said Emma.

Alex picked up a long stick and gave one to Ben. The boys carefully marked where the walls of their fort would go.

"Look! I made four bricks!" said Emma.

"Cool. Keep going."

"I don't want to."

Alex sighed. Emma always bailed.

"Come on, Ben," he said. "Let's make the bricks."

One by one, the boys filled the containers and piled the finished bricks. When they had enough bricks for their snow fort, they started to build. They built a front entrance to the fort near Alex's back porch.

By one o'clock grey clouds filled the sky, and they had more than half of their fort finished. They needed to build a wall and the back entrance and then they could crawl into their fort.

"I'm starving," said Alex. "Let's go inside for a quick sandwich."

The boys leaned their shovels against the house, piled their containers against the side wall of the back porch and raced inside. They flung off their hats, wet from sweat, and laid them out on the back door bench. They shook the snow off their boots, hung up their jackets and dashed into the kitchen.

"Peanut butter with jam and bananas?" asked Alex.

"Great," said Ben.

Ben's dad had gone home. Alex's family was watching an old movie in the living room.

"It's going to be an awesome fort," Ben said to Alex as they spread peanut butter and jam onto their bread.

"Yeah," said Alex. "It's . . . hey, did you hear that? It sounds like . . . It can't be. Not now."

The boys stopped smearing peanut butter onto their sandwiches and raced to the window.

The sun had completely disappeared. The clouds had turned a dark, gloomy grey and icy pellets pinged against the window.

"What do we do now?" asked Ben.

"Maybe it will stop. Come on. Let's try to keep building anyway."

The boys dashed outside to inspect their fort. The icy rain came down harder. Their damp hats got wetter.

"I'll grab the shovels and containers," said Alex. He hurried to the side of the porch. But as Alex reached for a shovel, he slid on a patch of ice.

His right leg twisted beneath him. "Ouch," he groaned.

"Are you okay?" asked Ben. "Can you stand?"

"I . . . I think I can . . . "

"Come on. Grab my hands and I'll yank you up."

With Ben's help, Alex hoisted himself up. Then he leaned against the wall of his house.

"Are you okay?" asked Ben.

"My leg hurts but I'll be okay."

Alex hobbled over to a mound of snow. Ben followed. The boys dug their shovels into the snow, but everything was so wet all they hit was slushy ice. They couldn't make good snow bricks from that.

And Alex's glasses were smeared with rain. He could barely see.

"I hate freezing rain," said Ben.

"Me, too. I can't see a thing."

"And my hands feel like icicles even with these thick gloves."

Alex sighed. "We'd better go in."

The boys trudged inside. They slipped off their boots and wet, dripping jackets. They shook out their drenched hats and gloves. Underneath, their hair was soaked.

Alex's mom hurried over with towels. "I was about to call you in. Give me your jackets and hats and I'll run them through the dryer. Then I'll make you hot chocolate to warm up. I don't think the freezing rain is going to let up for a while."

"I thought there was only a thirty percent chance of freezing rain," said Alex.

"And it was supposed to come down late in the afternoon," said Ben. "Not at one thirty. So much for weather reports."

Alex sighed. "Yeah. Our fort could have been great."

CHAPTER SIX

The next morning the temperature rose and the icy rain turned to a steady drizzle. Alex stared out of the window of his room. Their fort was turning into a sad mess. He and Ben were going to a movie. That would take their minds off their fort.

By Monday the snow on the streets and roads had completely melted. At school Mr. Moore talked about global warming and how it was making the weather yo-yo from heavy snow to warm temperatures and back again to snow and cold.

In the news, the local rangers and the national park service warned that the crazy weather might trigger more avalanches in the backcountry.

For the next two weekends, Alex and Ben

played video games and watched movies. Sometimes it was even dry and warm enough to play catch outside. Every time they got together they also drew snow fort designs. Each one had two entrances. Some had three storeys, four rooms and couches made of snow.

"I wish I had a snow-making machine," said Alex. "Then we could make snow forts even if it didn't snow."

"That would be awesome," said Ben.

"Look," said Ben's dad, showing them his phone. "The long-range weather report predicts snow next week. Well a sixty percent chance of snow, but that's pretty good. That's good news for the resort, too. Business has been down this month."

Alex closed his eyes. *Please let it snow,* he thought. *Let it snow and snow and snow!*

* * *

As soon as Alex walked into class on Monday, Owen glanced his way, poked Nate in the arm and whispered. Owen turned to Lena, whose desk was beside his, and whispered. Then he turned to Ryan, Sophie and Ethan and whispered.

No matter what he does, I am not going to let Owen bother me, Alex told himself.

But it was hard. Owen's whispers turned into loud comments. "Do you know how to ski, New Boy? It's going to be good skiing weather this weekend."

"I know how to ski a little," said Alex.

"On the bunny hill? Like this?" Owen stuck out his arms, wobbled and then slid to the classroom floor. "Oh dear," he said in a high-pitched voice. "I hurt my little self. My little bunny rear is sore. Can you help me stand up, Nate?" Nate extended his hand and yanked Owen up. Owen, Nate and Lena laughed. No one else laughed, but some of the kids gave each other looks. The only person who spoke up for Alex was Sophie.

"Stop it, Owen," said Sophie, glaring at him. "Not everyone knows how to ski."

"I'm just imagining how Alex would ski."

"Yeah, right." Sophie made a face at Owen.

Just then Mr. Moore walked in. Owen raced to his seat in the front row. As he passed Alex, he mouthed, "Bunny Boy" and wiggled his nose.

Alex tried to concentrate on *Forever Jones*, the book they were discussing for English. He liked the book, and last week he had contributed to the discussion. But he couldn't today. He didn't feel like doing anything today. If only he wasn't in the same class as Owen.

"Take out your journals, class," said Mr. Moore. "I'll give you twenty minutes to write. Remember: don't just write what you've been doing but how you feel about what's happening around you and to you." Alex tried to concentrate on his journal. He wanted to write about how Owen made him feel. But Mr. Moore sometimes read their journals. Alex didn't want to mention Owen. What if Mr. Moore said something to him? That would be worse.

Alex looked up at the clock. Ten minutes to recess. Alex's stomach churned. He was sure Owen was going to bother him at recess.

The bell rang.

"Come on," said Ben. "Let's play catch."

"I don't feel like going out. I . . ."

"Don't let Owen get you down," Ben whispered.

"I'll try," said Alex. "But he's not going to stop teasing me. He doesn't call *you* New Boy in that snarky voice. Just me."

"He'll stop. He'll get tired. Don't let him know that he bothers you. There was a kid like Owen in my school in LA. He teased me about my hair. He called me Goldilocks."

"What did you do?"

"I didn't know what to do at first. Every time he called me Goldilocks, I cringed. But then he said it once in this weird, creaky voice, and I couldn't help it — I laughed. He was so surprised that he stopped. From then on, every time he called me Goldilocks I laughed. Soon he found someone else to pick on."

"Okay. I'll try laughing."

It didn't take long for Ben's laughing theory to get tested. As soon as the boys hit the playground, Owen shouted. "Don't trip, Bunny Boy. You don't want to hurt your bunny knees. You'll need them for skiing the bunny trail."

Alex felt his face turn red. Bunny Boy was worse than New Boy. He took a deep breath and tried to laugh, but the laugh came out like a croak.

Owen stared at Alex. He covered his ears and wrinkled his nose.

"What weird sounds you make, Bunny Boy," he said. "You can't ski and you can't laugh. What can you do?"

"I may not be a good skier but I know about snow. I build amazing snow forts."

"Yeah, sure." Owen poked Nate in the side and the two of them laughed.

"If you don't believe me, come over and see." As soon as he said that, Alex wanted to yank his words back. He didn't want Owen coming to his house to see his fort. He didn't want Owen coming over for anything.

"I might just do that. My great-aunt and uncle live next door to you."

CHAPTER SEVEN

The recess bell rang. Alex and Ben ran inside. Soon Alex was so busy with a math quiz and a science experiment that he forgot about Owen.

At noon the bell rang for lunch.

"Look, Alex," Ben pointed to the window. "It's snowing — hard."

Thick snowflakes blanketed the yard. "If it keeps coming down like this, we'll have enough snow for a snow fort!" said Alex.

The snow didn't stop. By the time the last bell of the day rang, the snow covered everything — cars, trees, roofs, even the crossing guard's hat.

"I can't wait. Our fort's going to be awesome," said Alex as he and Ben ran out the front door.

"If this snow keeps up, we'll have enough snow

on Saturday to make two forts!" said Ben. "See you tomorrow."

Ben waved and headed toward his house. He lived a few blocks from the school. Alex hurried onto the school bus and slipped into a window seat behind Emma.

Emma turned around. "Are you going to build a fort on the weekend?"

"Yeah, on Saturday. That is if the snow keeps up."

"I'm playing with Lisa on Saturday, so I can't help you make bricks. But I can help if you build your fort on Sunday. I like making snow bricks."

"You do not. You only made four bricks last time."

"You used them. Next time I'll make more. You'll see."

Alex rolled his eyes. He was glad he didn't have to count on Emma or even his dad to help build. Ben would build with him. It had been fun to work side-by-side on their first fort, and it would have been amazing if it hadn't been ruined by the rain. This time they'd finish their fort. Alex closed his eyes and imagined what it would look like.

But to Alex and Ben's disappointment, it stopped snowing that night and it didn't snow on Tuesday or Wednesday. By Wednesday morning the weather suddenly turned warm, and Monday's snow began to melt.

"It doesn't look like we'll have enough snow for even a mini fort," Alex told Ben as the last bell of the day rang on Thursday. "The weather report said there's only a thirty percent chance of snow today."

"Remember last time? They don't know everything. Look!" Ben pointed out the window. It had started snowing lightly, but the snowflakes were so big you could see each one's beautiful pattern.

By the time the boys headed out the front door of school, the snow was coming down hard and thick.

"Fingers crossed this snow keeps up," said Alex as the school bus drove up. "If it does, do you want to come over on Saturday and build?"

Ben nodded. "Yeah. And I'm crossing my fingers, my toes and my eyes to make sure that it does."

To Alex's delight, it was still snowing when he

got home. It was still snowing while he ate dinner, worked on his homework, played a video game and climbed into bed.

Best of all, it was still snowing when he woke up. It had snowed so hard all night that there were little snow hills all over the yard.

There was enough snow now for a fort for sure. And the forecast predicted even more snow Friday night and flurries Saturday morning. This time they had to be right!

Alex was so excited about building a snow fort that when Owen called him Bunny Boy at morning recess, he really did laugh.

"What's so funny?" snarled Owen.

"Bunny Boy is a funny name," said Alex.

"It's not funny. You can't ski."

"So what? Come on, Ben, let's plan our fort."

"I bet you can't really build a good snow fort," Owen called after them.

"We can. Our fort will be awesome!" said Alex.

CHAPTER EIGHT

On Saturday at nine, Ben's dad drove up to Alex's house. The snow had eased off to flurries but it was still cold and crisp outside. Alex's house, the trees and Mount Ava shimmered in white.

"I'll pick Ben up at five before it gets dark," said Ben's dad.

"Come on, Alex. We'd better start our fort right away," said Ben.

"It's going to be great."said Alex.

"I'm sure it will be wonderful," said Alex's mom. "Don't forget to wear your hats and gloves. It's cold out there."

"We'll be fine, Mom. Really. Don't worry," said Alex, putting on his jacket and snow pants.

"My mom was a worrier, too," said Ben. "But in

LA, she didn't have to remind me about my hat or gloves."

"Yeah. Welcome to winter and snow."

"I like the snow, especially the kind that's good for forts. Let's build!"

The boys raced outside and grabbed two sticks. They dragged their sticks through the snow to outline the fort.

"Let's build two entrances," said Alex.

"And make our fort wider and higher than last time," said Ben.

The boys started filling their containers with snow for bricks. By eleven o'clock they had enough bricks piled near the side of Alex's house for half of their fort. Then they started to build.

At eleven thirty Alex's mom popped outside. "What a terrific fort, boys. I'm driving Emma to her friend's house and then Dad and I are going shopping. I told the Henshaws that we're out. They promised to look in on you."

"Come on, Mom," said Alex. "Don't worry so much. We're almost twelve. We can stay by ourselves for a few hours."

Alex's mom patted his arm. "You're right. But Mr. Henshaw said he'd love to see your fort. We'll be back by four thirty. See you soon."

At twelve thirty Mr. Henshaw snowshoed over. "Just checking that you boys are okay. And I brought you some of Mrs. Henshaw's chocolate cupcakes."

"Thanks," said Alex. "I love Mrs. Henshaw's cupcakes."

"Me, too." Mr. Henshaw smiled and surveyed their fort. "I used to build snow forts when I was your age, but never one as good as this."

Alex and Ben beamed.

"We're not far away, so call if you need anything." Mr. Henshaw waved and headed back to his house.

"Hey," said Ben. "I'm hungry."

"Let's finish this wall and we'll have more than

half the fort built. Then we can have lunch. We can have the cupcakes when we're finished building."

"Perfect!"

The boys added more bricks to the side wall of

their fort then hurried inside for lunch.

"Let's eat quickly. We should finish before dark," said Alex. "Tomorrow we can have lunch in our fort. It could be a fort and an ice hotel."

Twenty minutes later they were hard at work again. They were so busy building, they didn't see Owen clomp over in snowshoes.

"So this is your amazing snow fort?" he said. "My uncle was raving about it." Owen stood with his hands on his waist and scanned the fort from top to bottom. He walked around and around it, checking the fort from every side.

Alex and Ben ignored him and kept working.

Owen peered into an entrance. He tapped the side of one wall. He stood back, stroked his chin and stared at the fort as if he was about to give it a grade.

"Okay. I admit it. Your fort is actually pretty good, Alex."

"Thanks," said Alex. It was the first time since

he'd moved to Glory that Owen had called him by his real name.

"Look. It's boring at Uncle George's place. All he wants to do is play chess. I hate chess. I thought that maybe you guys could use some help. Uncle George thought so, too."

"Help?"

"Building your fort."

"I don't know, Owen . . ."

"I'm sorry for calling you names at school, Alex. So what do you say? Can I help?"

Alex looked at Ben. He knew they were thinking the same thing. It was going to be hard finishing the fort before dark without help. And maybe if they worked together, Owen wouldn't be such a pain at school.

"Okay. But it's our fort. You have to build it our way. Deal?"

"Deal."

Alex handed Owen a container and a shovel.

"Fill this up, pat the snow down and you've made a brick. Stick it on top of the brick pile near the house over there. We need more bricks for the last wall."

Owen filled a container with snow, tapped it down and turned it over beside the house. "Hey, look at this, guys. Good one, right?" Owen pulled his phone out of his pocket and snapped a picture of his snow brick. Then he took a picture of the fort.

Alex and Ben smiled. "Good one, Owen."

"Yeah. This fort is cool," said Owen.

Ben and Alex exchanged quick looks. Then they got back to work.

For the next hour the three boys worked steadily. Alex and Owen worked side-by-side shaping and piling bricks near the side of the house. Ben worked at the fort near the back porch. He placed bricks on the last wall and patted each brick down with his hands and his shovel.

The fort grew taller, wider and stronger by the minute.

"Hey! Maybe we could even climb into the fort today," said Alex. "We might finish by four if we keep working like this."

"That would be awesome," said Ben.

Alex walked over to a new mound of snow. He bent over to dig his shovel in and his glasses fell off. As he scrambled to find them, he heard a boom.

"Did you hear that?" he asked Owen.

"Yeah. I heard something. They're probably dynamiting near the road. They do that to stop avalanches from crashing down near the highway."

"That boom isn't down the road. It's close. Really close. It's like thunder. It's like . . ."

Alex squinted up at Mount Ava. "Owen! Ben! Look!" His heart began to pound.

A huge slab of snow thundered down the steep mountain. It snapped branches. It rammed into trees. It buried everything in its path and it was heading right for them!

"Avalanche!" shouted Alex. "Run!"

But it was too late to run.

Waves of heavy snow crashed over them, knocking them off their feet, tossing them like pieces of furniture, burying them under its heavy, cold weight.

And then there was silence.

CHAPTER NINE

Alex struggled to open his eyes. They felt heavy and cold as if someone had covered them with an ice pack. It hurt to blink. When he did, snow fell off the top of his lids and onto his nose. His nose felt like an ice cube stuck to his face. It felt like bricks were pressing against his chest.

Where am I? Where are Ben and Owen?

Alex shivered. He suddenly remembered the avalanche — the mountain of snow hurtling at him. Tossing him like a football. Tumbling him over and over till the snow finally stopped moving. Everything had happened so quickly.

Avalanche. Even the word made his heart beat faster.

It really happened. Here. In my own backyard.

But he was alive! He could breathe but it hurt. And he was cold. So cold.

He gagged and coughed. His mouth was full of snow. He swallowed some and it made his throat hurt. Icy bits scratched his throat. He spit out as much of it as he could.

How long have I been lying here?

Alex blinked his eyes open and shut. He wasn't sure which way was up. All he could see were smears of white and patches of blue. *Is that the sky?*

Alex tried to shake his head free from the snow. The snow on top of him felt so heavy he didn't know how he could move out from under it. *Come on. Get up!* he thought. *You have to get up. You have to move.*

Alex took a deep breath and tried moving his arms but only his right arm budged. And there was something in it. Alex jiggled it. It was cold, long and hard. *What is that?* And then he re-membered. He was holding his shovel when the avalanche hit. Somehow he still had it.

Alex wiggled his arm back and forth, knocking a little more snow off each time.

But it was hard to move the heavy snow. And he was suddenly so tired he just wanted to close his eyes and go to sleep.

No! Don't. You have to try.

With all his might Alex forced himself to knock off more snow. He wiggled his arm again and again, knocking chunks of snow with each movement till finally he freed his right arm, his hand in his soaked right mitten and his shovel.

His arm ached like he'd been lifting weights for hours, but it was free. And the metal shovel was a little dented but that's all.

Now the left arm. You can do it.

Bit by bit Alex pushed the shovel back and forth until he scraped snow off his left arm. Finally it too was free of snow, but he'd lost his left mitten in the snow and his wrist throbbed. He tried moving it but a sharp jab of pain shot through him.

Another wave of exhaustion hit him. It was like he'd been running all day. He wanted to close his eyes. Sleep.

Stay awake. Move! Get up. Find Ben. Find Owen. What if they're buried?

Alex tried to call out to his friends, but all that came out of his mouth was a croak. He cleared his throat and tried again.

"Ben! Owen!"

His voice was weak, raspy. He called their names again and again. His throat hurt but he kept calling as he pushed his shovel back and forth against his chest. He pushed over and over until his chest was finally free.

He tried to sit up. Pain shot through his arms and chest, and he fell back in the snow. His left wrist throbbed like a toothache, but he forced himself to sit up.

Alex took a deep breath. Breathing didn't hurt

as much now. He shivered as the cold pierced through his wet jacket and snow pants.

"Get off me, snow!" he said out loud as he kept pushing and shovelling the snow off his legs, until first his right leg, then his left leg were free. Luckily he still had his boots on. He touched his bare head. His hair was matted and wet all the way through to his scalp. His hat was gone.

He leaned on the shovel and with all his might yanked himself up. But as soon as he was upright, his head spun. He sat back down on the snow and held his head in his hands until the dizziness passed.

He called, "Ben! Owen!" No one answered.

Where are they? Why aren't they answering me?

The snow was so deep around him that it covered everything like a giant white blanket across a huge lumpy bed. It was hard to see clearly without his glasses, but he could see enough to get around. He could see the lumps of hard snow across his

yard and two of the trees in the back were broken in half. He could see the shed wrecked, smashed to bits. And his house . . . his house had caved in. The porch had been torn off.

Thank goodness no one was home, thought Alex. *Does anyone know what happened? Is anyone on the way to help us?*

Owen had been working near him piling bricks. Ben had been over at the fort near the porch. He had to get to them.

Alex called out to Ben and Owen again. Again no answer.

Alex swallowed a lump in his throat. He took a step and sank into a deep pocket of snow up to his knees. He lifted his legs and pulled himself out. He took another step and another, sinking into the hard, crunchy snow again and again. He stumbled on the chunks of football-sized snow dotting the yard. He kept calling for his friends. He tried to force his voice louder. But he was so hoarse, he couldn't.

"Ben! Owen! Are you there? Are you okay? Answer me."

And that's when Alex heard a faint croaking sound. It was close.

Owen! It had to be Owen.

CHAPTER TEN

"Owen!" Alex called, clutching the shovel and squinting.

He heard that croaking sound again. Closer this time. *Where is it coming from, the left or the right?*

Alex couldn't tell. He didn't know which way to go. The snow was so thick and deep each step took all of his energy. But he had to walk. Every moment counted for Owen and Ben if they were buried. Alex looked up at the sky. The sun was going down. It was going to be dark soon.

What time is it? Alex knew that his parents were due back at four thirty. And Ben's dad was coming to get him at five o'clock.

I wish I had a phone. Owen had a phone! But where is Owen?

Another croaking sound. Louder. Clearer. Closer. From the right. Alex was sure of that now. Alex took a few steps to the right. He sank into a pocket of soft snow. He took another step. And another. The snow was crustier here and he could walk over it, but it was lumpy, too. It was like walking over snowballs. He stumbled. His knees buckled. He fell into a rut in the snow. He lay there for a moment, catching his breath. As he forced himself up, a wave of dizziness and nausea hit him. He stopped to let the wave pass.

There's that croaking sound again. Close. Very close. There in a mound of snow, Alex spotted a dark green hat. Owen's hat!

Alex took another step and sank into the snow up to his waist. He crawled forward on his hands and knees, sinking and falling. He stood up and used the shovel to propel himself forward.

His arms hurt. His legs hurt. His face, his feet, his throbbing wrist. Every part of him was cold.

More waves of dizziness washed over him. But he kept going until he finally reached Owen's hat. Alex leaned down and brushed the snow off the hat.

Owen's face was under his hat! He was lying face up and he was breathing. He was alive. Only a thin layer of snow covered his mouth. Alex brushed the snow away from Owen's mouth, nose and eyes. Owen's eyes were closed. His breathing was heavy. Alex pushed the shovel into the snow beside him careful not to poke Owen with it.

"Owen!"

Owen opened his eyes. He blinked. He spit out snow from his mouth. He gagged and coughed. "Help me," he muttered. Alex brushed more snow off Owen's face. He grabbed the shovel and gently removed snow from Owen's arms. Then he shovelled his middle. Then his legs. "Can you stand?"

"I . . . I . . . don't know. I feel sick. And my chest hurts."

"I'll help you. Lift your arms. I'll help pull you up. Do you have your phone? We need to call for help."

"I had it in my pocket. I can't reach it."

"Let's get you up first."

Owen stretched his arms out. Alex grabbed them.

"Careful. I think I may have cracked something in my chest. Every time I breathe it hurts."

Alex pulled Owen and Owen, leaning on Alex, pulled himself up, too. Owen bit his lip as he stood up. Both his gloves were gone but he still had his boots on.

"Thanks," Owen muttered. "Ugh. I feel sick." Owen leaned away from Alex and threw up into the snow. He wiped his mouth with snow.

"You're going to be okay. You can walk. That's good. Do you have your phone?"

Owen touched his pocket. "I did. Right here. I don't feel it now."

"We have to look for your phone so we can call for help."

Owen reached deeper into his pocket. He checked his other pocket and the pockets in his jacket. "My phone's gone. It has to be here somewhere." He tapped the snow beside him. Nothing.

"Where is it?" said Owen. Alex dug in the snow around them. The snow near them was hard. It was like digging through bricks. There was no sign of Owen's phone.

"It has to be here. It has to," cried Owen. "Oh no! Look over there!" Owen pointed to his Uncle George and Aunt Wendy's house. "Their house is destroyed. They're in there — somewhere under the snow!"

Alex touched Owen's arm. "I know. But we're too far away to reach them through this snow. Keep looking for your phone so we can call for help. I'll look for Ben," said Alex.

CHAPTER ELEVEN

Alex trudged through the thick, heavy snow toward his broken porch and house. It was hard to see distance without his glasses but he could see right in front of him. He called, "Ben! Ben!" over and over until he was hoarse. Icy tears dribbled down his face.

What if we can't find him? Alex had to keep himself from thinking the worst. He had to keep looking for his friend.

Alex stopped to rest and as soon as he did, he felt shaky and dizzy. For a minute he thought he might faint but the feeling passed. He tried to move slowly. He took deep breaths. His head still spun but not as much.

Banks as high as his waist forced him to crawl across hard-packed snow as he carefully inspected the snow for any sign of Ben. His arms scraped against broken boards from his house, sharp edges of his porch screen, jagged table tops and parts of chairs, but there was nothing anywhere that belonged to Ben.

Where is he? It's getting late. Alex shivered.

"I found my phone!" called Owen. "I've tried it but it's all wet. It won't work."

"Someone will come soon, even without us calling for help. They know we're here. Someone has to know what happened here. There are other houses not too far away."

"But what if the whole neighbourhood has been hit?" said Owen. "The power is probably out. I can see downed wires from here."

"They'll find a way to get here. I just wish they weren't taking so long. We have to find Ben now. He doesn't have much time. If he's buried deep he might be . . ." Alex couldn't say the word *dead*, but the word kept pushing its way into his head.

"Hey! I found your glasses. Well, part of them anyway." Owen held up Alex's glasses. One of the black arms was missing. The lenses were cracked.

"Thanks! All this squinting is giving me a headache. Help me look for Ben. You can see better than me now."

"I'm coming." Owen coughed. "My chest is killing me. It's like someone is stabbing me every time I move or breathe."

Owen trudged over to Alex and handed him his glasses. "Can you see through them?"

"If I hold them, I can. Not perfectly but it helps. Can you see anything around here that belongs to Ben?"

Owen picked up a large board from the remains of the porch and looked under. There was no sign of Ben underneath.

Alex lifted up a broken wooden tabletop that used to stand on his porch. Ben wasn't under there.

Where is he? He has to be here.

And then Alex saw a red dot in the snow. It wasn't far from the caved-in remains of their fort and a long board from the shed, which covered the entrance to what was left of the fort.

Is that blood?

Alex shuddered. His heart raced as he tramped over to the red dot. He put on his glasses to inspect it. It didn't look like blood but he wasn't sure. He slipped his glasses into his jacket's top pocket and shovelled the snow near the dot. He crouched down and dug some more. There was more red and some black.

"It's Ben's glove! Ben has to be close," he called to Owen. Alex dug more around the glove. Nothing. Nothing. And then he hit something hard and rubbery. It was the bottom of a boot!

Alex dug frantically near the boot. Owen stumbled over.

"Help me. I think Ben is here."

Owen bent down beside Alex. Together they

dug with their hands and with the shovel. "It's Ben's leg! Come on. We have to uncover his face. Hurry!" yelled Alex.

"What if . . . ?" whispered Owen.

"We can't think about that. We have to get him out," said Alex.

The boys kept digging. They dug with their hands until they uncovered Ben's face. His shovel was up against it, his hand holding the shovel tightly. There was a deep gash across his forehead. He was breathing, but each breath came out hard, as if it hurt.

Alex leaned over his friend. "Ben, it's us. You're okay. We found you." Alex carefully unclasped Ben's fingers from the shovel and gently pulled the shovel away from his face so he could breathe better.

Ben's face was bruised. His nose and lips were cut. His eyes were closed, but for an instant he opened them and blinked — once, twice. Then he closed his eyes again and moaned.

The boys kept digging until they removed most of the snow off Ben's arms, legs and chest.

"Let's not move him," said Alex. "He might have broken something and moving him might make it worse. Someone will come. Your mom, Ben's dad. My parents. Someone. They are all due back soon."

"I hope so. Ben's shivering," said Owen. He sat down on the snow beside Ben. "He's having trouble breathing."

"We have to keep him warm," said Alex. He moved closer to his friend. "My jacket is too wet and so is yours. I wish we had a blanket."

"Wait! I have something." Owen slipped off his wet jacket. Underneath he was wearing a long, thick sweater. "Aunt Wendy knitted this for me for Christmas." Owen paused and looked toward the Henshaws' house. He coughed. Tears filled his eyes. He wiped them away quickly with the back of his hand. "Mom made me wear this today because we were visiting. It's ugly but it's dry."

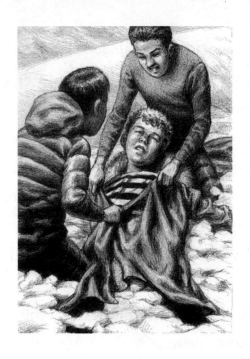

Owen placed the sweater over Ben and tucked it around him. Then they settled in close to keep him warm. Ben blinked. He moaned. He coughed. Then he closed his eyes as if the pain was too much. Alex and Owen could hear his short, sharp breaths.

"You know, I used to live here," said Owen. "Before my parents split up."

"Alex's eyes widened. "You lived here? Did you

sleep in the attic beadroom?"

"Yeah. Living in town's okay, but I kind of miss my old life."

The boys were quiet for a few minutes.

"The sun's going down. It'll be dark soon." Alex shivered. "And it's getting colder. My feet are like ice."

Owen nodded. "My chest is so sore it hurts to yawn."

"Maybe one of us should walk to the road — or what's left of the road."

"I can't move anymore. I'm too tired and my chest hurts too much. Plus we should stay with Ben."

"You're right," said Alex. "We can't leave Ben."

Alex looked over at Owen. He was leaning against Ben. His eyes were closed. He was sound asleep.

Alex closed his eyes.

I'll just rest for a few minutes, too. Only a few minutes. Maybe then . . .

CHAPTER TWELVE

"Alex! Alex! Can you hear me?"

Alex opened his eyes. A young woman with flaming red hair was standing over him as she and a man lifted him onto a stretcher. As they carried him over the rutted, lumpy snow in his yard, a jolt of pain shot through him. Each bump made him wince. Everything ached. But help had arrived!

"Thank you," he muttered.

"My name is Arlene. You don't have to talk. You and your friends have been through a lot."

"Are they okay?"

"Your friend Ben is on his way to the hospital. We moved him first. He needed the most attention."

"Will he . . . ?"

"His condition is very serious, but it looks like we got to him in time. Your friend Owen said you two dug Ben out. You may have saved his life."

"Where's Owen?"

"He's on his way to the hospital, too. Both of you were asleep when we arrived." Arlene grinned. "Avalanches are exhausting."

"You're not kidding," said Alex.

"Just lie back and take it easy. It's going to take us a while to transport you to the hospital. The roads are in bad shape. Debris, wires, trees and lots and lots of snow are blocking the road. This avalanche took the whole town by surprise."

"Do my parents know?"

"They know you're okay. The road coming in is closed, so they're meeting us at the hospital. Go ahead, rest, Alex." Alex closed his eyes. There was a warm blanket around him. He was still cold but he wasn't shivering. He was so tired but he was safe. Ben was alive. He was breathing. And Owen was okay, too.

* * *

The next thing Alex knew he was in a bed in a pale green room.

A nurse was standing beside him, checking his pulse. "My name is Nancy. How do you feel?"

"Woozy. Tired. My wrist hurts like crazy." He looked at his left wrist and noticed the cast.

"You broke your wrist. That's why they put it in a cast. You're not left-handed, are you?"

Alex shook his head. He looked down at the cast around his wrist. "I don't remember anyone putting this on."

"You were dazed when they brought you in. Are you still dizzy and nauseous?"

"A little, but not as bad as I was right after the avalanche."

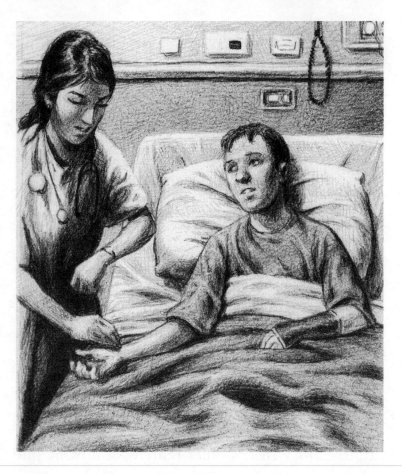

"Can you sit up? I'll help you." The nurse leaned
over and put her arm around Alex's shoulders. She
gently helped him sit up. "How's that?"

"Better."

"Maybe resting helped, although it's hard to rest

in a speeding ambulance with shrieking sirens. And it's a bumpy ride."

"I don't remember the ambulance. I don't even remember arriving here. Where are my parents?"

"They've been here the whole time. They just stepped out to make some calls. I finally convinced them to go out and stretch their legs. They were incredibly worried about you and your friends."

"Are my friends okay?"

"Your friend Owen is next door resting. He was awake when they brought him in. He can tell you more about how he feels soon. Your friend Ben is being observed in the ICU. We're observing you and Owen too, you know."

"I'm okay, except for my wrist and some bruises. Why do I need to be observed?"

"You could have a concussion. We'll keep you here overnight to check you out. Don't worry. The food isn't as bad as they say. How about some water?"

"Thanks." Alex gulped the water down. He hadn't

realized how thirsty he was. He handed the cup back to the nurse as his parents and Emma walked in.

His mother and father rushed over to hug him. Emma took his hand and squeezed it.

"We're so relieved you're okay," said his mom. "What a nightmare."

"Yeah. It was scary," said Alex. "The avalanche came out of nowhere."

"But you and your friends made it through," said his dad. "That means everything."

"Did you see Ben?" asked Alex.

"Not yet. His dad is with him in the ICU. The doctors are taking good care of him," said his mom.

"Will he be okay?"

"They're very hopeful," said Alex's dad.

"Can I see him?"

"You need to stay in bed and rest. The doctors want to be sure you don't have a concussion."

"I'm better. Please, I want to see Ben. I'd feel a million times better if I saw him."

"Me, too."

Alex looked up. Owen, in a green hospital gown like the one Alex was wearing, was standing at his door.

CHAPTER THIRTEEN

"I asked my mom to find out about Ben but the doctors wouldn't tell her much either," said Owen. "Mom's checking on Aunt Wendy and Uncle George."

"We'll talk to Ben's dad and let you boys know what we hear. Try not to worry," said Alex's mom rubbing his back. "How are your aunt and uncle, Owen?"

"Not great. Uncle George is badly bruised and they said he has hypothermia from being out in the cold, so they're keeping him warm. He was buried in the snow, but he had an air pocket near his face when the avalanche threw him near a broken board."

"And your aunt?"

Owen's lip quivered. His eyes suddenly filled with tears. He wiped them away and looked down at the floor. "Aunt Wendy wasn't breathing when they found her. They revived her but she's . . . she's on . . . a breathing machine now. They don't know if she'll make it."

"Oh no. I'm so sorry, Owen." said Alex's mom. "Please tell your mother that we're here to help in any way we can. Your uncle and aunt have been so kind to us."

"Your uncle always hurries over when we have any problem with the house," said Alex's dad. "And your aunt brought over a casserole the first night."

"And remember how she always makes extra meatballs and brings some for me 'cause I liked them so much when they invited us for dinner?" said Alex. "And she made us cupcakes just before . . . the avalanche." Alex bit his lip. It hurt to think of Mrs. Henshaw.

"Their house is destroyed," said Owen. "We don't

know where they're going to live. We don't have room. We only have a small apartment in town."

Alex's dad nodded. "I know. Our house is gone, too."

"Where are we going to live?" asked Emma.

"For now we'll stay at the resort. My manager has arranged everything."

"I'm glad that my real bed is back in Halifax," said Emma. "But my toys and my books and the doll house Grandma bought me for my birthday are in our house here. And now . . ." Emma began to cry.

Her mom hugged her. "We've lost a lot of stuff, Emma. But we have each other."

Emma wiped her eyes on a crumpled tissue from her pocket.

"Look," said Mr. Mason. "It's dinner time. Let's head down to the cafeteria and get something to eat. Do either of you want anything from the cafeteria? I know they'll serve you dinner but we can grab you something, too."

"I'm not hungry," said Alex.

"Me neither, but thanks, Mr. Mason."

"Okay. We'll be back soon."

As soon as Alex's family walked out, Owen sat in the chair beside Alex's bed.

"I have an idea," said Alex. "Let's go to the ICU and find out about Ben before the nurse gets back to your room."

"They might not let us in. I bet they only let in family."

"But we're Ben's friends. That's almost like family." Alex slipped off the bed and stood up.

"Okay," said Owen. "Let's go. But we both look weird in these green gowns. I have to keep tying mine so it doesn't open in the back."

Alex tried tying his gown tighter but it was hard with a cast on his wrist.

"Here. I'll help you," said Owen.

"Thanks."

Owen tightened Alex's gown. "I can't tell which

side of these gowns is the front or the back. I asked the nurse and she said it didn't matter."

"Both ways look dumb," said Alex.

"I know. Keep checking your gown. We're going to get a lot of laughs if they're open."

Alex smiled and took a step. Then he stopped.

"Are you still dizzy?" asked Owen.

"No. Just getting used to walking again. Come on, let's find the ICU."

The boys peeked down the hall. There was only one nurse at the front desk. Her eyes were glued to her computer. She didn't look up as they tiptoed down the hall to the elevators.

"Which floor?" asked Owen.

"I don't know. Let's ask this man."

A hospital orderly was pushing a patient in a wheelchair down the hall. "Which way to the ICU, please?" asked Alex.

"One floor up," said the orderly. "Unit C."

The elevator opened. The orderly rolled his

patient inside and Alex and Owen joined them.

Alex and Owen stepped out on the third floor.

"This way," said Alex pointing to a sign and an arrow.

"Wait a minute. You need tightening again," said Owen as they reached the double doors of the ICU.

"Oops. They might not let us in if my gown is open."

"They might not let us in no matter what. Look." Owen pointed at a button next to the doors. A sign above it read "Push to request admittance."

Alex pressed the button.

"Yes?" said a nurse. "Can I help you?"

"We're here to see Ben Green. We're his friends."

"I'm sorry. Mr. Green can't have visitors except for immediate family."

"But we won't bother him. We just want to see him for a minute. We want to know how he's doing."

"Do you know his father? Why don't you speak to him? He was just here."

"Where is he now?" asked Alex.

"He stepped out for some fresh air."

"Can you tell Ben that his friends Alex and Owen were here to see him?"

"I'll see that he gets the message," said the nurse.

CHAPTER FOURTEEN

"Where were you?" asked Alex's mom. "We came back and you were gone. One fright a day is enough for me."

"Owen and I went to the ICU to see Ben," said Alex.

"They didn't let you in, did they?" asked Alex's dad.

"No, and they wouldn't tell us anything either. They said we had to ask Ben's dad."

"We just saw him in the elevator. Ben's conscious but his breathing is still shallow. He has a bad case of hypothermia and they're keeping him warm. He also has frostbite and a broken ankle but they won't operate on his ankle until he's stable."

"But he'll be okay, won't he?" asked Alex.

"He hasn't spoken yet and they're worried about

the trauma to his brain. They're monitoring him."

Alex bit his lip. He didn't want to cry. Not in front of Owen, his parents or Emma. But the news about Ben wasn't good. He could tell from the expression on his parents' faces that they were worried about him, too.

"You look much better," said Alex's mom.

"I feel better. I want to go home. Well, home to the resort. Let's ask the nurse if I can leave. Please."

As if on cue, Nurse Nancy marched in with a tray of food, medicine and a thermometer.

"Did I hear something about my patient wanting to go home?" she asked.

"Yes. I'm much better."

"You do look better but I'm afraid we're going to have to keep you here overnight. If you continue to improve, we'll kick you out by early afternoon tomorrow. Here's a tray of food I put aside for you."

Alex lifted the metal cover on the tray. Mac and cheese, green beans and applesauce.

"Is it any good?" he asked.

"It's gourmet." Nurse Nancy's eyes twinkled. "Well, maybe not gourmet. But it's not bad for hospital food."

"I hate green beans," said Alex.

"And I won't tell the chef if you don't eat them. I'll be back in twenty minutes to take your temperature. Make sure you're still in bed, Alex. I hear you've been wandering around the hospital."

Alex's eyes widened. "How did you know?"

"Word gets around fast here. And I have my spies." Nancy winked at Alex.

"Are you Owen's nurse, too?"

Nancy laughed. "Yes. And Owen was late for his ice pack. He confessed that you two had been trying to break into the ICU to see your friend."

"We didn't break in. We pushed the button and asked to visit him. But the nurse wouldn't let us in."

"Well, I have some fast-breaking news about your friend in the ICU."

Alex's heart began to pound. "What is it?"

"Ahhh, here's the man who can tell you himself."

Alex looked up. It was Ben's dad.

"Dave. What are you doing here?" asked Alex's dad.

"How's Ben?" asked Alex.

"Better! He just started talking a few minutes ago. He recognized me. He asked about you, Alex. The nurse told him you and Owen were trying to see him."

"That's great news," said Alex.

"I wanted to come and thank you and Owen for digging him out. They tell me you saved his life."

Alex blushed.

"It may be a while before Ben's back to normal," Ben's dad continued. "He's still a bit confused and he doesn't remember what happened. He knows there was an avalanche but all he can remember is this mountain of snow coming at him."

"When will they move him out of the ICU?"

asked Alex's mom.

"They want to monitor him further. He's got bad frostbite on his left hand. He lost his gloves in the avalanche but we're hoping he doesn't lose . . . a finger." A streak of pain crossed Ben's father's face. "But his breathing is better. The doctors think he's going to be all right."

"That's the best news ever!" said Alex.

"I also came to ask you and your parents if you'd consider staying at our place until things settle down."

Alex's eyes lit up. He looked at his parents.

"That's very kind, but we wouln't want to impose," said Alex's mom.

"Nonsense. I'd welcome the company. And I know that when Ben's feeling better, he'll need someone to help him build another snow fort."

The thought of building again with Ben made Alex smile.

CHAPTER FIFTEEN

On Thursday morning Alex got ready to return to school. But it felt weird to be going back. His stomach churned like the first day of school in September.

So much had changed. He'd had to rest at home after being released from the hospital on Sunday. He'd had nightmares every night about snow crashing through their house and burying them. Each time, his parents rushed in to find him sitting up in bed shivering. His mom, read to him until he finally fell asleep.

For the last five days when he'd woken up, his first thoughts were of Ben. He'd been allowed to visit him in the hospital for the first time on Wednesday, but they'd only let him stay for ten minutes. Ben smiled when Alex walked in but he hadn't said much. He was still weak. He was having surgery next week for his ankle. Alex promised he'd come every day to visit. That made Ben smile again.

Alex and his parents had visited Mr. Henshaw in the hospital, too. Sadly, Mrs. Henshaw hadn't made it. She was too weak to survive her injuries.

Mr. Henshaw was getting better but he was having a hard time accepting that his wife was gone and that the house they'd lived in for thirty years was a pile of bricks, metal and wood. How could life change so fast?

* * *

"Have a good day," said his dad, pulling up to the front of the school.

Alex walked down the hall to his class. The bell was about to ring. As he neared his classroom, one of the kids shouted, "Hey, let me see that article!"

"Wow. Our class is famous," called another kid.

"I'm glad an avalanche didn't hit my house," said a third.

As soon as Alex walked into the room, he was surrounded.

"Hey, Alex. Welcome back. How's Ben?" asked Sophie.

"He's better," said Alex.

"Did you read the article?"

The *Glory Chronicle* had run a front-page article about the avalanche on Monday. But a reporter had interviewed Alex and Owen on Tuesday for a longer feature article.

"Not yet."

"Here." Sophie thrust a copy of the day's paper into his hand. "You're big news!"

Alex scanned the headline: The Avalanche That Shook Glory. Before he could read more, Mr. Moore walked in, the bell rang and the kids scurried to their seats.

"Welcome back to class, Alex and Owen. We're all relieved that you're both on the road to a full recovery. I've also just spoken to Ben's dad and I'm happy to report that Ben is on the mend, too. He had a rough time but he hopes to be back at school in a few weeks. We'll have to open a lot of doors for him since he'll be hobbling around on crutches."

"We can do that," called out Sophie.

"Great. I thought I'd start the day by reading the article in today's *Chronicle*. Then we can talk about avalanches, why they happen and what you do in case you're caught in one. We can also ask our new avalanche experts for their take on the subject." Mr. Moore smiled at Alex and Owen.

Then he began to read:

No one can imagine that on a bright, sunny February day an avalanche will roar down a mountain, hit your home, your friends, your neighbours and you. That was the case for three Glory kids, Alex Mason, Ben Green and Owen Slater, who were happily building a snow fort Saturday afternoon. Everything was going well. The thick, slightly wet snow was just right for a fort. The sun was shining on Mount Ava, behind the Masons' house. There wasn't much wind.

"It was a perfect day to build a snow fort," recalls Alex. "Then we heard this terrible sound. When we looked up, we saw the avalanche coming straight for us."

There was little time to run or take cover. The avalanche thundered down the tall, jagged mountain straight toward Alex, Owen and Ben, destroying two homes and smashing the snow fort the three boys had so carefully constructed.

"It happened so fast, I couldn't think straight,"

said Owen Slater.

A combination of luck, knowledge and quick thinking saved the three boys' lives.

Alex Mason was lucky the avalanche hadn't buried him deeply in the snow. He was lucky that he'd recently read about avalanches and knew how crucial it was to act quickly to dig out anyone buried in the snow. He still had the shovel he'd used to build a snow fort and used it to dig himself out and then rescue his friends.

Owen Slater was lucky Alex spied his green hat in the snow and dug him out quickly. Both boys knew that despite their injuries, they had to move quickly to find their classmate, Ben.

And Ben Green, who was buried the deepest and longest in the snow, was lucky that Alex discovered his red and black glove peeking out from the hard-as-cement snow. Ben was especially lucky that his shovel landed on top of him and created an air pocket so he could breathe. He was lucky that his friends *knew to keep him warm until help arrived.*

Ben is now recovering in hospital. Unfortunately the avalanche resulted in one fatality: 68-year-old Wendy Henshaw, the beloved wife of George Henshaw and Owen's great aunt.

A snowboarder inadvertently triggered the Mount Ava avalanche on Saturday. The Town of Glory has now posted permanent and visible signs alerting all winter sports enthusiasts that the mountain is off limits. The Town also plans to erect a snow structure as soon as possible to protect homes below Mount Ava and ensure that a tragedy like this never happens again. It's the first time an avalanche has struck private homes, and the Glory community hopes it will be the last.

Mr. Moore put the newspaper down. "You boys have had a harrowing time. We're proud of you for knowing what to do, acting quickly and standing by one another in a terrifying situation."

The class burst into applause.

Alex blushed.

Owen grinned. "Yeah, it was pretty scary being buried alive. And we didn't know when help

would come." Owen glanced at Alex. "But we helped each other get out alive."

Alex smiled at Owen. "Owen's right. It was lucky we were there for each other. I don't want to go through another avalanche again."

"But before the avalanche we almost built a good snow fort, didn't we, Alex?"

"Yeah. And next time we'll finish our fort. And it won't get knocked down. Not by anything!"

"Even if it doesn't get knocked down," said Sophie, "you know it will melt when the weather warms up."

Everyone laughed.

Alex looked around the room and smiled. It felt good to laugh with his classmates. He and Owen had become friends, and Ben, would re-cover soon.

Glory finally felt like home.

Author's Note

Looking up at a mountain when it's covered with snow takes your breath away. Being caught on a mountain in an avalanche is terrifying.

Avalanches occur all over the world. Most affect climbers and skiers in the backcountry, far from the groomed ski trails. Skiers and climbers who venture into areas known for avalanches often risk their lives.

Experiencing an avalanche at ground level is rare but it can happen. It happened on February 28, 2014 in a suburb of Missoula, Montana, in the Northern Rockies. Some homes in the community were built close to Mount Jumbo, which had never been a problem until the day a snowboarder entered a restricted area on the mountain. He set off an avalanche that roared down the mountain, destroying a few houses and killing one person.

I set *Avalanche!* in a town like Missoula. I called my fictional town Glory and placed it in an area of British Columbia surrounded by the Rockies and the Selkirk Mountains and close to national parks like Jasper, Glacier and Yoho. It's a region that often has avalanche warnings, even along highways.

Avalanche in Missoula, Montana, 2014

In my story I also mention an avalanche that buried gold prospectors in the Yukon's Chilkoot Pass in 1898, during the Gold Rush. Some prospectors ignored the warnings that weather and snow conditions made an avalanche possible. About sixty people were buried as the snow crashed down.

Today climbers and skiers carry equipment such as air bags, probes, ropes, transceivers and shovels, which help save the lives of those caught in an unexpected avalanche.

~Frieda Wishinsky

Facts About Avalanches

- An avalanche occurs when a large slab of snow moves swiftly and suddenly downhill. It can be caused by a combination of heavy snowfall, few trees, an earthquake, strong vibrations, steep slopes, wind and changing weather.

- People trigger 90 percent of avalanches.

- Wherever there are high mountains, there is a chance of an avalanche. In Canada avalanches occur most frequently in British Columbia, Alberta and the Yukon. Other regions that have experienced avalanches are Quebec, Newfoundland and Labrador, Nunavut and the Northwest Territories.

- Professional avalanche workers sometimes

set off explosives, artillery shells and pro-pane blasts in areas with unstable slopes in order to prevent avalanches.

- About 90 percent of avalanche victims sur-vive if they are dug out within 15 minutes. After that time the survival rate falls sharply. Lack of oxygen is the greatest threat to life. Hypothermia and frostbite are big factors in injuries.

ALSO AVAILABLE

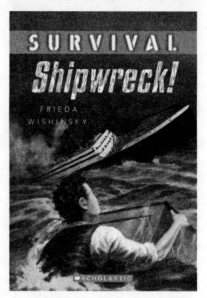

ISBN 978-1-4431-4641-8

Albert and Grace feel a jolt. The ship begins to tilt. People scream. Stewards order passengers to head for the lifeboats. Water rushes into the ship as passengers race to the top deck. The ship tilts toward the water. Lifeboats crash down. Grace and Albert have no choice. They leap into the St. Lawrence River.